PIG, HORSE, OR COW, *Don't Wake Me Now*

Story and photographs by ARLENE ALDA

A Picture Yearling Book

Published by
Bantam Doubleday Dell Books for Young Readers
a division of
Bantam Doubleday Dell Publishing Group, Inc.
1540 Broadway
New York, New York 10036

ISBN: 0-440-41226-9

Reprinted by arrangement with Doubleday Books for Young Readers

Printed in the United States of America

August 1996

10 9 8 7 6 5 4 3 2

For Emilia and Scott
Who I love a lot

With special thanks to
Beverly, Lynn, Amy, Alan,
and Harry and Peggy Schleiff.

Once upon a summer morn
A peacock woke and called for corn.
He honked and cawed his special sound.
He spread his tail and turned around.

The peacock's voice woke up a pig,
Whose ears and snout were very big.
The fat and grumpy piggy said,
"Oink-oink, who got me out of bed?"

The oinks woke up a calf next door
Who wondered what the noise was for.
She mooed and mooed with all her might
And gave the lamb a dreadful fright.

The lamb heard “Moo” and woke up fast.
She thought that breakfast time had passed.
She looked around and said, “Baa-baa,
I’m hungry now, but where’s my ma?”

The lamb's baa-baa got duck upset.
He didn't want to wake up yet.
He opened up his mouth to yawn,
But out came, "Quack—can it be dawn?"

A horse got up when he heard "Quack."
The morning sun was on his back.
He stamped his hoof and whinnied, "Neigh,
I guess I'll eat some grass today."

The neigh, it seems, woke up a cat
who got confused—now, fancy that.
She took a walk and said, "Meow—
Was I supposed to wake up now?"

The cat meowed and purred a lot.
She woke a boy whose name was Scott.
Scottie said, "What made me wake?
I'd like more sleep, for goodness' sake."

Scottie loved his cozy bed.
He loved the dreams inside his head.

His mom came in to start the day.
"The cat is up; she wants to play."

"Uh-uh," said Scott. "I'm having a dream
About a dog who loves ice cream,

And of a hippo in deep water,

And of a baboon with her daughter."

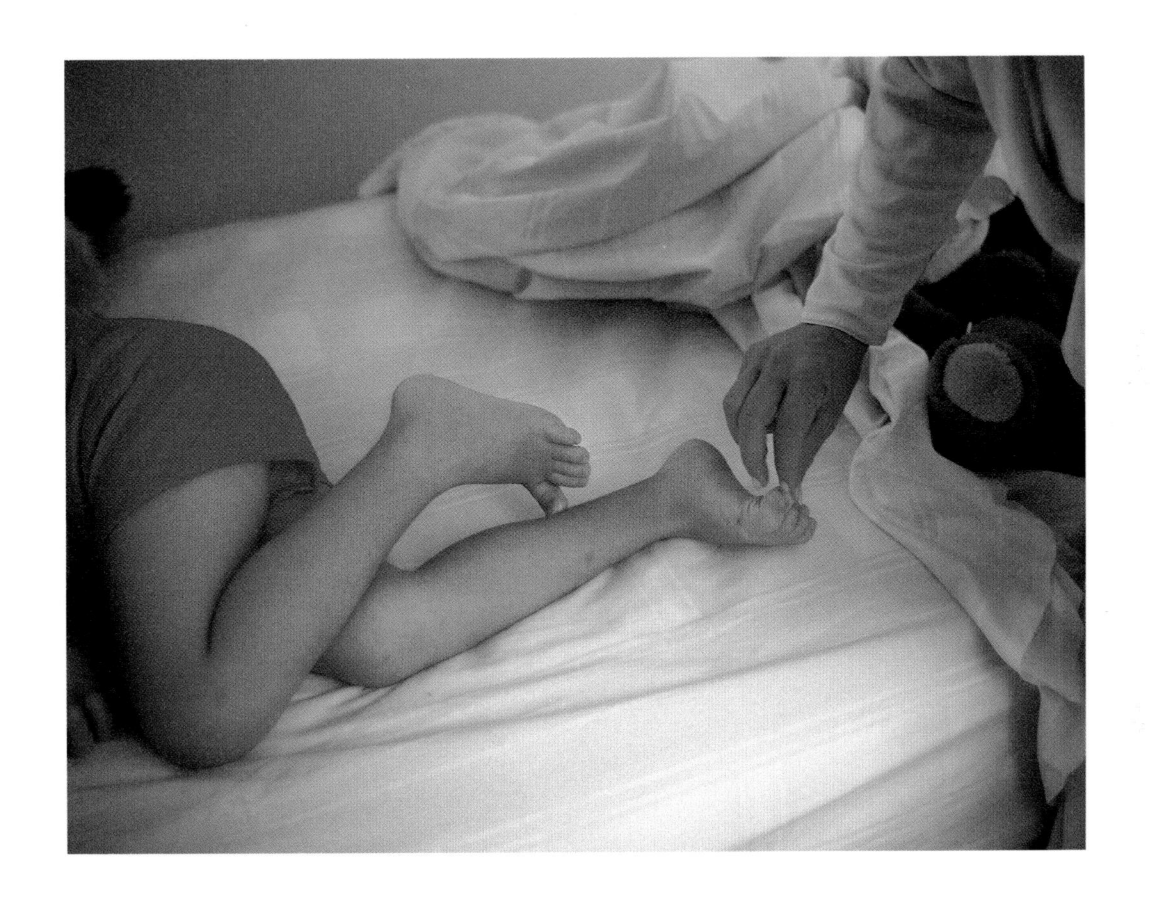

Mom pulled on his blanket and tickled his toe.
"One to get ready... two to go."
Scott giggled and wiggled but still stayed in bed.
Mom thought for a moment. Here's what she said:

"Let's race down to breakfast. I bet I'll win."
"I bet you won't," said Scott with a grin.
He suddenly sprang like a horse on the run.
He leaped like a lamb. His sleeping was done!

He screeched and he squawked as he flew down the hall.
His mother was shouting, "Be careful; don't fall!"

He got down to breakfast with no time to sit.
He gulped down his juice and nibbled a bit.

Scott looked at his mom. He was happy, of course...
Then he ate like a pig and chomped like a horse.

And so ends the story of that summer morn
When peacock awakened and called for his corn.